Little
HORRORS

Shiver with fear...

Owwl!

...shake with laughter!

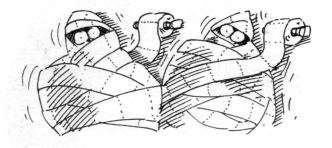

Visit Shoo Rayner's website!
www.shoo-rayner.co.uk

ORCHARD BOOKS
96 Leonard Street, London EC2A 4XD
Orchard Books Australia
32/45-51 Huntley Street, Alexandria, NSW 2015
First published in Great Britain in 2003
First paperback edition 2003
Copyright © Shoo Rayner 2003
The right of Shoo Rayner to be identified as the author
and illustrator of this work has been asserted by him in
accordance with the Copyright, Designs, and Patents Act, 1988.
A CIP catalogue record for this book is available
from the British Library.
ISBN 978 1 84362 011 2 (paperback)
5 7 9 10 8 6 (paperback)
Printed in Great Britain

Little
HORRORS
The Bogey Man

Shoo Rayner

ORCHARD BOOKS

I was terrified!

My sister, Kim, and I were riding the Galaxy Orbiter at the funfair. We were spun around, turned upside down, thrown way up high, then dropped to the ground.

When the ride was over, we
staggered out. I was nearly sick.

I clutched my stomach and heard laughter. Some friends from school had been watching us.

"Ha! Ha!" laughed Jamie. "Didn't you like the little merry-go-round?"

They all climbed on to the Galaxy Orbiter and had a great time, laughing and whooping all the way round.

Kim and I didn't want to go on any more wild rides, so we went on cups and saucers.

It was great fun, until Jamie and his friends came along and called us names.

They made me really angry!

When we finished, Jamie said, "We're going on the ghost train...you coming too?"

"Yeah!" I said, without thinking.
Then my stomach lurched. I don't
like being scared.

The outside of the ghost train was covered with badly made models. Dracula! Frankenstein's Monster! Ghosts! Ghoulies! Mummies! Monsters!

The largest model was over the
ticket office. Underneath was
written, "The Bogey Man!"

Over the grim entrance to the
tunnel, there was another terrible
sign.

I didn't like the look of it.

Jamie slapped me on the back.
"You're not scared, are you?"
"Of course not!" I laughed
nervously.

A man sat inside the gloomy
ticket office, reading a book. His
hair was long and wild…like the
model of the Bogey Man.

He took our money. In a very creepy voice he told us to get in the train, keep our hands inside the carriage and watch out for the Bogey Man!

Big foam bars pinned our shoulders back and locked us into our seats.
We couldn't escape!

I need not have been scared.
The ride was pathetic!
Dracula's teeth were falling out.

Frankenstein's monster's stitches
were coming undone.

The ghosts and ghoulies were just old sheets flapping about on string.

The mummies looked like they were wrapped in toilet paper.

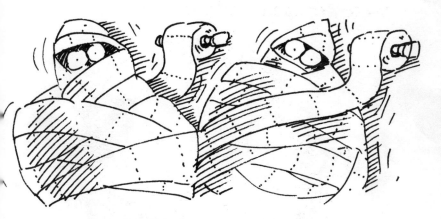

We didn't see the Bogey Man.

When the ride finished, Jamie went to complain at the ticket office.

"It's the Bogey Man's afternoon off," said the attendant.

"Well, when does he start work again?" Jamie asked sarcastically.

The attendant leered, "Tonight, seven-thirty sharp." His eyebrows quivered. One of his eyes was green and the other was blue!

"Right," said Jamie. "We'll be back. Just wait and see!"

Walking home I said, "I'm not sure about going back tonight."

"You're not scared of the Bogey Man, are you?" laughed Jamie.

"N-n-n-no!" I said. "It's just that Kim and I might be busy."

Jamie wasn't having any excuses.
He taunted me until we agreed to
meet everyone at the ghost train at
seven-thirty, sharp!

It was dark when we got back to the fair. Now, the flickering lights made the models on the front of the ghost-train building look a little bit scary.

"Th-th-they almost l-l-look alive,
d-d-don't they?" stammered Kim.

"It's just a trick of the lights," I said,
trying to calm her. But she was
right…they did seem to be moving!

Only Jamie came. All of the others had chickened out.

The attendant glowered from the ticket-office window.

"So! You've come to see the Bogey Man, have you. Hop in…it's free tonight!"

It was like a different ride. Kim screamed as Dracula swooped. Blood dripped from his sharp teeth!

Frankenstein's monster loomed over us. Jamie almost squeaked.

I was attacked by ghosts! Not old sheets on bits of string…these were light and filmy. They seemed to pass right through me, chilling the blood in my veins.

Screams and alarms shrieked!
A hideous, bellowing laugh rattled
my bones.

Red lights flashed. Terror glittered in Jamie's eyes...then everything stopped and the lights went out!

There was only silence - and the dark - and the bars that held us trapped in our seats!

Jamie whimpered. "A-a-a-re you two OK?"

"Y-y-y-yes!" I said, through chattering teeth.

"N-n-n-no!" squeaked Kim.

We waited…

With a grinding squeal, the bars lifted up over our heads, setting us free.

"Come on," hissed Jamie. "Let's get out of here. Follow me."

We stumbled towards the sound of the fair. Jamie lifted a curtain and we saw the exit.

The last few ghosts and monsters were just sheets and plaster models, but the flickering lights of the fair still made them look spooky.

"We never saw the Bogey Man," said Kim.

"Oh yes we did!" Jamie sniggered. "The attendant was picking his nose when we arrived!"

Laughter drove away our fear. We wanted to tell the attendant what we thought of his stupid ride...but he'd gone...disappeared.

The ticket office was dark. The door was locked and the window was closed.

"What a cheat!" said Jamie. "There's no such thing as the Bogey Man."

We stood there, wondering
whether to get hot-dogs or candy
floss. I looked above the ticket office
and saw that the model of the
Bogey Man had gone!

The lights flashed on again. All the other models seemed to come alive, staring crazily!

Alarms screamed. The rail tracks shook. The train rattled out of the tunnel.

Something was driving…something wild and hairy…eyes blazing…green teeth grinning madly. It threw back its head and laughed maniacally.